Level **2**

The Nature Kid's Guide to

LIZARDS

DAVID ANDERSON

LP Media Inc. Publishing
Text copyright © 2026 by LP Media Inc.
All rights reserved.

For information address LP Media Inc. Publishing,
30012 Variolite St NW, Princeton MN 55371
www.lpmedia.org

Publication Data

Lizards
The Nature Kid's Guide to Lizards — First edition.

Summary: "Learn all about Lizards, the Nature Kid Way"
— Provided by publisher.

ISBN: 979-8-89818-213-7

[1. Lizards – Non-Fiction] I. Title.

Title: The Nature Kid's Guide to Lizards

CONTENTS

LIZARD LEGENDS

Skitter! A tiny collared lizard darts across the hot sandy ground.

Lizards live all over the world. You can find them in hot deserts and wet rain forests. Some even live near the sea and swim in the ocean!

Lizards come in many shapes and sizes. Some lizards are as small as your thumb. Others grow bigger than a grown-up! There are more than 6,000 kinds of lizards on Earth, and scientists keep finding new ones.

Lizards have been here for a very long time. They were here when dinosaurs walked the land. These tough animals are still going strong today.

SCALY SECRETS

Some geckos have no eyelids — they lick their own eyeballs to keep them clean!

Scratch! A gecko grips a rough tree trunk with its tiny claws.

A lizard's body is built for life in the wild. Most have four legs, a long tail, and skin covered in tough scales that work like a suit of armor. Sharp claws help them grip and climb rocks and trees with ease.

Many lizards can drop their tail when grabbed by a **predator**. The tail keeps wiggling on the ground, distracting the enemy while the lizard escapes! The tail slowly grows back over time.

Lizards also have surprisingly sharp eyes. Most can see in full color, which helps them spot food and notice danger before it gets too close.

SUN BATHERS

FUN
FACT!
Desert lizards do push-ups to lift their belly off sand to cool off when it gets super hot!

Sizzle! A marine iguana stretches flat on a warm rock in the hot sun.

Lizards are **cold-blooded**. This means their body does not make its own heat. They need the sun to warm up.

On cool mornings, lizards **bask** on rocks in the sun. Once warm, they can run, climb, and hunt. If they get too hot, they move to shade to cool down.

That is why many lizards live in warm places. Deserts, jungles, and sunny shores make great homes for these sun-loving reptiles.

STAY SAFE

The horned lizard squirts blood from its eyes up to 5 feet to scare enemies!

Puff! A frilled lizard swells up big and wide to scare away predators.

Lizards have many ways to stay safe. Some blend in with leaves and bark so well that predators walk right past them. They hold perfectly still and wait for danger to pass.

Others try to look scary instead. Some puff up their bodies, spread flaps of skin, or flash bright colors to look much bigger and more terrifying than they really are. A lizard that looks dangerous is a lizard that gets left alone!

Some lizards are built for speed. They run fast to escape danger. A few can even leap from branch to branch high in the trees.

KOMODO KINGS

FUN FACT!

A Komodo dragon can gulp down 80 pounds of meat in one meal — bones and all!

12

Thud! A massive Komodo dragon stomps through the forest.

The Komodo dragon is the biggest lizard on Earth. It can grow up to ten feet long and weigh over 150 pounds! That is heavier than most grown ups.

These giant lizards only live on a few small islands in Indonesia. They hunt deer, pigs, and even water buffalo. One bite can make **prey** very sick from their venom and germs.

Komodo dragons flick their long, forked tongue to smell the air. They can sniff out food from miles away. These powerful hunters rule their island homes.

CHAMELEON CHAMPIONS

The smallest chameleon fits on your fingertip and is tinier than a grape!

14

Zap! A chameleon's sticky tongue shoots out and grabs a bug in one snap.

Chameleons are famous for changing color. They can shift from green to brown, yellow, or even bright blue! They change color to show mood or talk to other chameleons.

These lizards move in a slow, funny way. They rock back and forth like they are on a boat. Their eyes can look in two directions at once, so nothing sneaks up on them!

A chameleon's tongue can be twice as long as its body. One quick flick, and lunch is caught in less than a second.

FAKE LEAVES

This gecko opens its mouth wide to flash a bright red inside and scare attackers!

Shhh! Can you spot the lizard hiding in those leaves?

The leaf-tailed gecko looks just like a dead leaf. Its flat body and bumpy tail fool other animals completely. This tiny lizard lives only in the rain forests of Madagascar.

During the day, it sits very still on branches. Birds and snakes look right past it! Its brown, leafy shape keeps it safe from hungry predators.

At night, this gecko comes out to hunt. It creeps along branches and catches insects with a quick snap. Big round eyes help it see in the dark.

OCEAN DIVERS

Baby marine iguanas must outrun fast snakes the moment they hatch — it is a race for survival!

Splash! A dark lizard swims in the cold sea. It's a marine iguana!

The marine iguana is the only lizard on Earth that swims in the ocean. It lives on the Galapagos Islands near South America. Every other lizard runs from the water. This one dives in for lunch.

These tough lizards plunge into cold water to munch seaweed off rocks. They can hold their breath for up to 30 minutes! Then they climb out and warm up on sunny rocks.

Marine iguanas sneeze out extra salt from the sea. It lands on their heads and makes them look crusty and white. They are truly one of a kind!

THORNY TRICKSTER

The thorny devil has a fake head on the back of its neck to confuse predators!

Crunch! A thorny devil snaps up ants one by one by one.

The thorny devil is covered from head to tail in sharp spines. It looks scary, but it is small and harmless. This little lizard lives only in Australia.

Thorny devils only eat ants. They sit near an ant trail and lick them up one at a time. One hungry thorny devil can eat 3,000 ants in a single day!

This lizard has a cool trick for finding water. Tiny grooves on its skin catch drops of morning dew. The water slides right to its mouth for a drink.

They can even change color with the temperature. In the cool morning it is dark brown. As it warms up in the desert sun, its skin turns a lighter yellow!

GLIDING DRAGONS

The mother draco lizard guards her eggs fiercely for exactly 24 hours after laying them. Then she climbs back up into the trees and never returns.

Whoosh! A draco lizard leaps from a tree and glides through the air.

The draco lizard is sometimes called the flying dragon, but it does not really fly. It glides! Long ribs stretch out flaps of skin on its sides. These flaps work like little wings.

These small lizards live high up in the forests of Southeast Asia. They glide from tree to tree to find food and escape danger. One glide can carry them over 25 feet through the air!

Draco lizards eat ants and small insects. They spend most of their life up in the treetops and rarely touch the ground. They come down only to lay eggs in the soil.

BLUE BLUFF

Blue-tongued skinks crunch and swallow snails whole — shell and all!

Bleh! A fat skink sticks out its bright blue tongue at a hungry hawk.

The blue-tongued skink has a big surprise inside its mouth. When a predator gets too close, it opens wide and hisses. Out comes a bright blue tongue!

The flash of blue scares many animals away. In the wild, bright colors often mean danger or poison. The skink is bluffing, but the trick works!

Blue-tongued skinks live in Australia. They eat fruit, snails, and bugs. Their short legs and round body make them slow, so a good bluff is their best defense. Unlike most lizards, they do not lay eggs. Mothers give birth to live babies, sometimes up to 25 at once!

FRILL FRENZY

DID YOU KNOW?

A frilled-neck lizard's frill can spread as wide as a dinner plate!

Pop! A lizard fans out a huge frill around its neck like a big umbrella.

The frilled-neck lizard has a big flap of skin around its neck. Most of the time, it lies flat against the body. But when this lizard is scared, the frill fans out wide!

It opens its mouth, hisses loudly, and stands on its back legs. Suddenly it looks much bigger than it really is. Most predators turn and run away.

These lizards live in northern Australia and New Guinea. They spend most of their day up in trees hunting insects. When they run on the ground, they sprint on two legs like tiny dinosaurs!

GILA GRIP

FUN FACT!
Gila monsters can survive for months on fat stored in their chunky tail!

Chomp! A Gila monster yawns after a long nap. He's hungry!

The Gila monster is one of the few venomous lizards on Earth. It lives in the deserts of the southwestern United States and Mexico. Its name comes from the Gila River in Arizona.

This heavy lizard is slow, but its bite is strong. Venom flows from glands in its lower jaw. It holds on tight and chews to let the venom work.

Gila monsters have bumpy skin in black, orange, and pink. They spend most of their time resting in cool **burrows** underground, waiting for their next meal.

SPOTTED STALKERS
FUN FACT!
Leopard geckos cannot climb smooth walls. They lack the sticky toe pads other geckos have!
30

Click! A leopard gecko chirps softly as it hunts its next meal.

The leopard gecko gets its name from its spotted skin. It looks like a tiny leopard! These geckos live in the dry, rocky deserts of Asia.

Leopard geckos come out at night to hunt. They stalk crickets, beetles, and spiders with patience. Their big eyes help them see with very little light.

Unlike most geckos, leopard geckos have eyelids. They can blink and close their eyes to sleep. Before they pounce on prey, they wave their tail slowly back and forth.

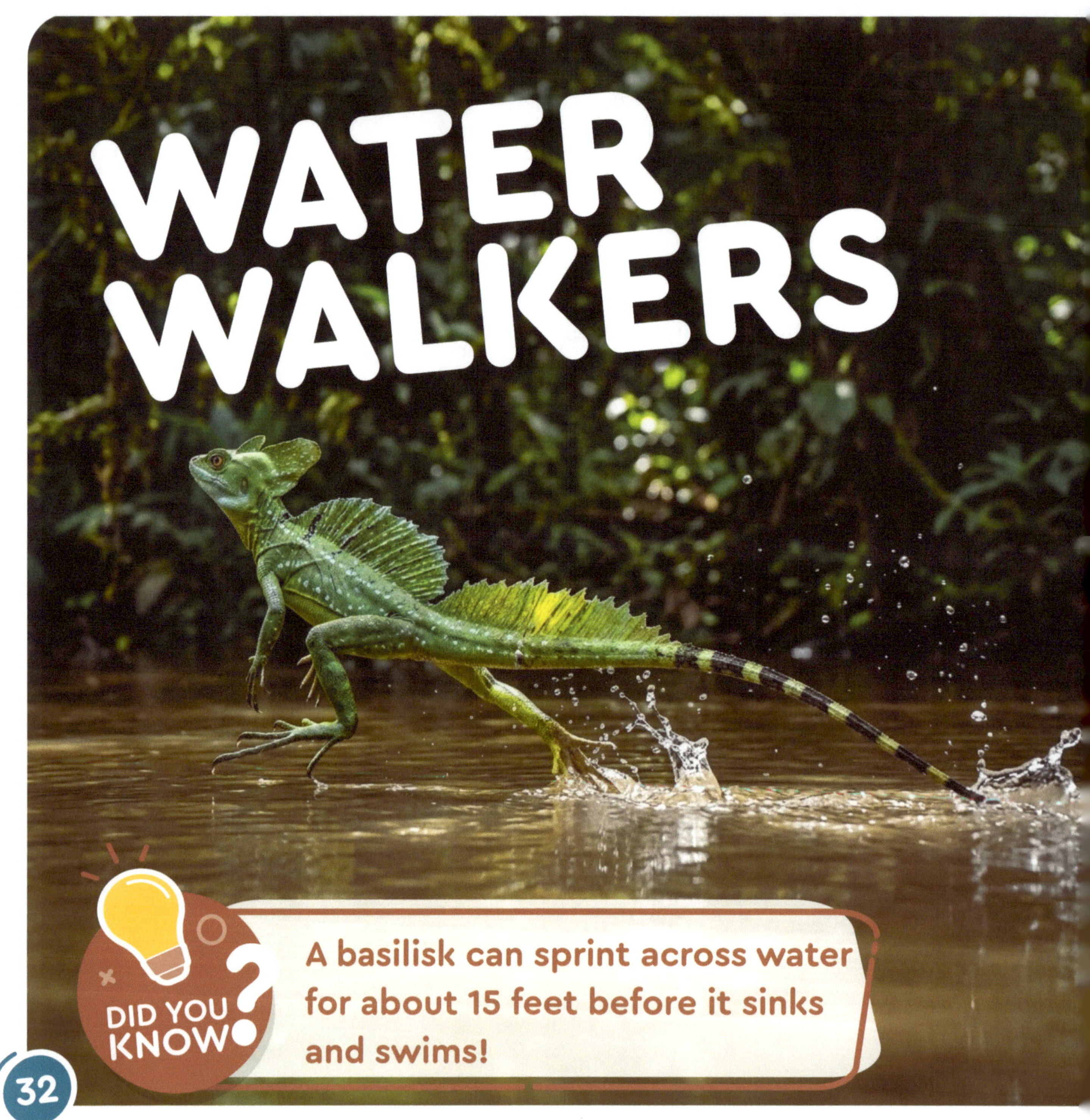

WATER
WALKERS
DID YOU KNOW?
A basilisk can sprint across water for about 15 feet before it sinks and swims!
32

Slap, slap, slap! A lizard races across the top of a pond.

The basilisk lizard can run on water! It slaps its big back feet down so fast that it stays on top. No other lizard can pull off this amazing trick.

Basilisk lizards live near rivers and streams in Central America. They rest on branches hanging over the water. If danger comes, they drop down and race across the surface!

These bright green lizards eat insects, flowers, and small fish. Their long tail helps them balance as they dash over the water at nearly 7 miles per hour.

ARMOR BALL

Armadillo girdled lizards live in groups of up to 60 — rare for lizards!

34

Curl! A spiny lizard rolls into a tight ball and bites its own tail.

The armadillo girdled lizard has a clever way to stay safe. When scared, it grabs its own tail in its mouth and curls up tight. Its spiny scales form a tough, round ball.

This trick keeps its soft belly hidden inside. Most predators cannot bite through the prickly armor. It looks just like a tiny, scaly donut!

These lizards live in the rocky lands of South Africa. They munch on insects and plants during the day. When the sun gets too hot, they rest in cool cracks between rocks.

LIZARDS LOST

Scientists discover new lizard species every year, but some go extinct before they are ever found. There may be lizards out there we never even get to name!

Crack! Old trees fall as the forest shrinks around a chameleon.

Many lizards are in trouble today. The biggest threat is losing their homes. When forests are cut down or wetlands are drained, lizards have nowhere to go and nothing to eat.

Cats, rats, and other animals brought by people eat lizard eggs before they can hatch. On islands like Hawaii and Guam, these newcomers have wiped out entire lizard species completely.

We can help by protecting wild spaces and keeping pet cats indoors. Learning about lizards matters too. Animals that people know and love are the ones that get saved.

LIZARD
LEGACY

FUN FACT!

The oldest lizard fossil ever found is over 200 million years old — older than most dinosaurs!

38

Rustle! A huge komodo dragon walks across the trail as tourists stop and watch.

Lizards make our world a better place. They eat bugs that can harm crops and gardens. They are also food for birds, snakes, and other animals in the food chain.

People are working hard to save lizards. Rangers guard wild places like Komodo National Park. Scientists study lizards to learn how to help them survive.

You can help too! Watch for lizards on your next hike. Tell your friends how cool they are. The more people who care about lizards, the more we can protect them.

GLOSSARY

bask

To rest in warm sunlight to heat up the body

burrow

A hole or tunnel in the ground where an animal lives

cold-blooded

Having a body that warms or cools with the air around it

predator

An animal that hunts and eats other animals

prey

An animal that is hunted and eaten by other animals